Unknown
Destinations

Unknown Destinations

EDWARD NEU, MD

Copyright © 2013 by Edward Neu, MD.

Library of Congress Control Number:		2013908791
ISBN:	Hardcover	978-1-4836-4107-2
	Softcover	978-1-4836-4106-5
	Ebook	978-1-4836-4108-9

All rights reserved. No part of this book may be reproduced or transmitted in any form or by any means, electronic or mechanical, including photocopying, recording, or by any information storage and retrieval system, without permission in writing from the copyright owner.

This is a work of fiction. Names, characters, places and incidents either are the product of the author's imagination or are used fictitiously, and any resemblance to any actual persons, living or dead, events, or locales is entirely coincidental.

This book was printed in the United States of America.

Rev. date: 05/17/2013

To order additional copies of this book, contact:
Xlibris Corporation
1-888-795-4274
www.Xlibris.com
Orders@Xlibris.com
134387

Contents

Prologue 7

Chapter One   A New Day Begins 9

Chapter Two   What If? 15

Chapter Three   The First Meeting: Life After Death 19

Chapter Four   Back on the Floor 26

Chapter Five   The Second Meeting: Reincarnation 28

Chapter Six   A New Day and Night 35

Chapter Seven   The Third Meeting: Time 39

Chapter Eight   A Quiet Day 47

Chapter Nine   Meeting Four: The Great Hall of Knowledge 50

Chapter Ten   An Unusual Day 55

Chapter Eleven   Reincarnation—Experiences of Life Between Lives 57

Chapter Twelve   Teaching Rounds—A Case Study 60

Epilogue 63

Prologue

Joe sat in the chair with it pushed up against the hospital bed, his hand holding Anna's. Her calm but slightly sibilant respirations and the beeping sounds of the heart monitor were the only noises in the room. The smell of antiseptic trying to cover the odor of the wounds was prevalent. He could feel a hushed silence from outside the room.

He was exhausted after his night before on call, when he used his learned life-saving abilities to do his best to save the poor souls who came through the emergency room doors in need of help. This work always exhilarated him because this was his calling—to intercede in an unnecessary shortening of an individual's physical life.

But here he was holding Anna's hand, completely incapable of using any of his physician's skills to help her condition. He felt helpless, unable to do anything but to be at her side.

As the fatigue started to overtake him, there was a change in the earlier rhythm of the monitor. He was having trouble keeping awake, staying conscious, but as he looked over Anna's bed, he saw an amorphous light and felt a lightness that he always had associated with Anna's essence. With this, he felt a pulling from his chest that made him feel that he should meet up with that light. With that pulling, in his exhausted state, he let go and started to float up above Anna's body, which still lay quietly on her hospital bed.

Anna met him and told him that though it was her time and she had done what her purpose was in this lifetime, he still had places to go and things to accomplish in his life.

Though, in his stuporous, sleepy delirium, he was in that light flowing from her center and was told not to follow but to move on with his path, his desire. He wanted to follow that dreamy, ethereal white light emanating from her upper body.

He was lifted up to that place where souls who passed on went. Anna was there, along with many souls of those he recognized who had gone before. There they told him that this time on earth was special and cannot be squandered and that he needed to return. Though he asked for an insight into his true purpose, he was given none. Instead, he was told that life here was a personal test, a trial that needed resolution. He was, at least, given the insight to know that this specific purpose for his life was still available but, as yet, unfulfilled. He also became aware that this purpose needed to be blind to him as that was the only way that his physical life, with the necessity of free choice, could be validated.

He was told to have the faith that his life would proceed in a way that his true purpose would have the best chance of coming to fruition. He was told that those who had gone before him, including Anna, would do whatever they could through guidance to help him fulfill his true purpose. With that, he began to become more aware of the intensive care setting with the beeping of the monitors, the smell of antiseptic, and the low buzzing of the subdued fluorescent lighting in the ceiling. He felt the support of the chair that he had been slouching in.

He was back, there at Anna's side, hand in hand, but it was clear that she was lifeless. The nurse entered the room to turn off the steady drone of the heart monitor and the intrusive pumping of the respirator. She looked at Joe but knew, as his eyes met hers, that his soul had somehow found peace.

Chapter One

A New Day Begins

The alarm went off at 5:30 AM. He was tired although yesterday had been only a Sunday ten-hour stint. Still, he wanted to get in to cover some loose ends and check some overnight results before medical rounds started at 7:00 AM.

He missed Anna last night, but she had to visit her family, and he didn't have the time or energy. So they agreed to crash separately.

Since waking, he ruminated about his life and was convinced that she was the one. They had known each other for just a short time, but he felt that she was the light that he was looking for. He enjoyed their discussions about life and was intrigued by her thoughts about one's purpose here. He had been raised in a traditional Catholic family, full of the belief that one was supposed to live life right or according to the laws laid down thousands of years ago and repeated in church every Sunday. Her ideas about other purposes were something to contemplate.

Getting himself up and ready was routine, but as he got into the car to drive to work, he remembered her discussion about the shell protecting the inner kernel as much as the car protected him from outside influences but allowed him to experience life outside of himself. He wasn't sure that he accepted all that she had to say, but a soul living inside of a physical body was an interesting supposition. After all, he was a man of science, and there was no scientific evidence for such thoughts. He was too busy trying to save the physical lives of these souls to think about what grander schemes may lay beyond this physical realm.

Some days, he would enter the hospital through the front door, but today he went his usual way through the emergency room. He wanted to see what may be waiting for him when his day shift started.

As soon as he passed through the sliding ER doors, he heard, "Hey, Joe, you have to come over and get a look at this."

It was his friend and fellow third-year medical resident Ravi. Ravi enjoyed doing some ER moonlighting work when he wasn't doing on-call work. "Rav, I don't know if I have time for this, but I'll take a peek." The patient was a teenage girl who had a couple of days of stomach upset and now was unable to control the muscles of her face. She had just come in and was lying on the gurney, obviously uncomfortable, with constant movements of her face including lip smacking. She seemed to be in a bit of respiratory distress as well.

"Give her fifty milligrams of IV Benadryl," said Joe. "That's tardive dyskinesia, probably from her taking Compazine for her nausea."

Once the nurse carried out his orders, the patient quickly returned to full control. Both she and Ravi thanked Joe for dropping by. Now he could get on to his business up on the ninth floor, his current home away from home, where he tended to spend seventy-plus hours a week, making sure that his patients got better and his junior residents became more knowledgeable.

He wanted to get to the floor before the night nurses left, because they could give him some insights on the last eight hours that he had missed. The delay in the ER set him back a bit, and he was able to catch up with only his favorite nurse, Mary, who had been tending to his most difficult patient. He thought about it briefly on the way up to the floor, but in this Catholic hospital that recruited many of its nurses from an affiliated Catholic nursing school, there seemed to be a good representation of nurses named Mary.

He hoped that the tea he picked up in the cafeteria on the way up to the floor would give him at least a five-minute sit-down with whom he felt was the best nurse on the floor. If you treated the nurses well, then life could be easier for you. They were, after all, even if a few years younger than him, professionals who had completed their training, and as a resident physician, he was, in a way, yet a student still learning his craft. He thought it strange sometimes that even at the age of twenty-nine, he was still what he would consider a student even if he was making a small stipend for his long hours. It was the learning that was still the main driving force for these residency years that he was going through.

The reality, as he saw it, was that even though the patients in the hospital had attending physicians who may have known them for years or been assigned to them as they presented to the emergency room, he and his team of a resident and an intern were the ones in the trenches, dealing with the ups and downs, twists and turns in these patients' courses. If a blood pressure dropped or a lab report showed a surprise, then his team was the first to act, and then they could fill in the attending physician later.

In a way, he felt that he was an extra appendage for the attending, who couldn't be everywhere at once. He remembered a patient who belonged to a physician whom he respected while he was the resident on call in the emergency room. When this patient, who had a history of migraines, came in with a headache, he went to evaluate her. The headache was debilitating, so the attending decided to admit her for observation. After talking to her, however, Joe heard that this was a headache that she had never experienced before. When he called the attending and got approval for a spinal tap, he made the diagnosis of viral meningitis, not a migraine. This was where he felt that he and his team of residents had to excel in—catching things that the attending physician couldn't catch, because his team had the eyes and hands on the patients while the attending physician couldn't be there.

Mary smiled when she saw him with the tea. He approached her and offered the tea. "Come over here, and sit down. I have a few updates for you," she said with an appreciative look. "And it is nice to see an alert, friendly face after a long, tiring night." They took a couple of seats in a corner cubicle at the end of the hallway.

The ninth floor was predominantly for medical patients but also held a few overflow surgical patients from the floor below. It was laid out in two long hallways containing four private and twelve semiprivate rooms each, for a total of fifty-six available beds. Joe's team, including a second-year resident and an intern, was one of two medical service teams on the floor. Each team took responsibility for twenty to twenty-five acutely ill patients while the remainder of the beds was used by surgical patients.

Mary took a sip of her tea and then started. "So I'll tell you about the easy ones first. The new one in 16B with the pneumonia broke her fever last night, so it seems the antibiotics that you chose were the right choice." Community-acquired pneumonia could be from a number of different organisms, and the cultures would take two to three days to identify the particular pathogen. For that reason, sometimes, one would treat with more than one antibiotic until lab results could narrow down the culprit.

It was easier sometimes, especially with new patients, to use their room number to bring up their case even though this, at times, seemed a bit cold, but in some ways, it could also just be a type of shorthand. "Mrs. Hendricks's leg infection in 13A seems to be improving finally after the antibiotic change." Again, after a person had been in the hospital for a few days, their names were more likely to be used.

"Your puzzle in room 2, though, Mr. O'Malley, still is slowly growing weaker and losing more sensation in his arms and legs despite anything we have done. His vital signs are still fine." Joe thought about this case for a couple of minutes. A list of possible diagnoses included a host of causes that could injure what was called the peripheral nervous system, which regulated control of both the muscles and sensations, such as touch and temperature. There were metabolic conditions such as vitamin deficiencies, diabetes, or infectious conditions that could set off abnormal responses in the body, and then there was the possibility of poisoning with heavy metals, such as arsenic. The labs were, so far, inconclusive as to a cause but gave further information showing irritation in the patient's liver as well. Hopefully, there would be more in this morning's lab report run.

"Puzzles" often were reasons to use a private room because of unknown causes of an illness, which could turn out to be infectious for others. Of course, other reasons for a private room were requests from a patient if he or she desired and could afford it and if a room was available or just the fact that the hospital was using all available beds, which happened frequently.

"Any change in Sally in 10B?" Joe asked. She had come to the emergency room via paramedics after having a stroke. That kind of a problem, though, in a person in her late thirties was unusual. X-rays on admission had shown the damage to her brain near the communication center in the right temporal lobe, but there was no sign of blockage in her neck arteries. Again, she had been at the hospital for only three days, and the esoteric blood tests looking for an unusual cause of stroke for an unusual patient were still a few days from being ready.

"She is still not speaking, but it seems that she can swallow a little thickened liquid now. I heard from her nurse that they tried a little gelatin-thickened juice early this morning after she wrote 'thirsty' on her pad." Mary seemed to be up on the patients on her floor even if they weren't her own. That was why Joe found these morning briefings useful. He also enjoyed those few moments of her company. Even though he was now in a new relationship that he was deeply committed to, he had known Mary longer and cherished their platonic, professional relationship. She was a definite asset to the hospital and to his ability to fulfill his residency training/teaching commitments.

"Hey, Joe, I've got the night's labs to go over if you're ready." It was his second-year resident, Paul, coming around the corner. Joe liked Paul's enthusiasm and energy. It was good to have a second-in-command like him. Paul could fill in on decisions when Joe was occupied elsewhere, but he could also ride the intern when she needed a little push. Sometimes Joe thought that Paul may be pushing her a bit too much, but Kate was a good intern and seemed to respond well to Paul's nudges. It really was a tradition in their training that there was a pecking order, that those who were one step up the ladder could push and be expected to teach the ones below them. It seemed that Paul didn't do it too much, and Kate appeared to respond to the generally good-natured bantering well.

Joe didn't really see much reason to apply the same teaching technique to Paul as he seemed to be sufficiently, inwardly motivated. His with Paul were more often presenting a new case or treatment quandary and asking for opinions regarding diagnosis and/or treatment options. From there, they could discuss a range of possibilities. The thrust in his educational training was to be sure that Paul or whomever he was working with at the time would not get fixated on one answer, because often, when one did not leave all possibilities exposed, the true answer to the problem could get missed.

Mary got up out of her cubicle seat. "I'll leave you guys to your business. I have to get home. Thanks for the tea, Joe. You two have a good day."

Joe responded, "You too. I'm covering the emergency room consults, but I'll stop by and see you tonight." His group was on call tonight, so they would be spending the next thirty-plus hours at the hospital. Usually, if you could get lucky and find two hours of sleep during the night, then you could handle the next day's chores.

Also, tomorrow afternoon would be teaching rounds with Joe's favorite teaching attending. These sessions lasted a couple of hours three days a week and were chances for the three of them to bounce thoughts off an impartial, specialized physician, who was committed to furthering their education. Joe particularly enjoyed Dr. Sub's methods because of his Socratic approach, which often led them to finding the answers for themselves rather than just presenting a case and getting feedback. Dr. Sub made them think, and with that was the sign of a good teacher. Joe often tried to use that method with those under him.

Joe commented, "Before I forget it, let's present Sally in 10B to Sub tomorrow. You can have Kate do it."

"Okay, that sounds like a plan," responded Paul. "But we still don't have any new labs on her. The immunoassays won't be back for a couple of days."

"That just makes it more interesting when we don't have an answer yet, doesn't it?" retorted Joe. "It would be boring to present cases that we already understand, don't you think? Teaching rounds are a time to look for extra input, and from Sub, we can get some good hematological insights."

Teaching rounds with Sub were always educational and stimulating. Whether large or small, a nugget of new information always seemed to be acquired. At the least, the time they spent was always interesting. And if Joe was learning something, then he was sure that the others in his crew were learning something too. These were the years to be sponges and to pick up as much knowledge, whether from the books or tidbits from the teachers' experiences, as they could. At times, the various residents on other services would also share interesting, unique cases on their watch so that everyone could learn from a rare ailment.

Reflecting at times, it seemed to be a strange but unique environment to Joe. No one but individuals in their situation saw so many incidents with people on the edge of their physical existence. Here, though, they were charged with the most solemn of duties, namely, to do all they could to return an ailing patient to health and, at times, save him or her from impending death. He found those encounters not only exciting and rewarding but also often thought provoking.

What was sobering about these encounters with patients at the edge of life crisis was that it didn't matter where they came from. Whether one was a CEO of a large company or someone living on the street, whoever they were, at that moment of time in their lives, they were all equal. All were souls who had spent time here on this physical plane and were possibly ending that existence to move on. Feelings expressed by these patients varied. Some were very fearful while others seemed to have an inner calm, and there was a whole range of emotions in between.

Because of some of these encounters, he couldn't totally dismiss Anna's conviction that there was something beyond this physical existence. The problem, though, was that he still found it a frustrating concept as it seemed essentially unable to be proven in a scientific environment.

He had, however, been doing a lot of thinking about these unknowns. He was considering talking with several of the current medical and even surgical residents about creating a recurring discussion group to probe and explore several questions about what could be beyond this physical life. He wondered if a look into the beyond could provide some insights regarding whether there truly was a purpose or meaning to life other than just to live and experience it.

He felt too that discussing some of the deeper questions of life could add a counterbalance to the pure physicality of life as he and his cohorts experienced it in the hospital setting. He decided to bring his ideas up with his crew the next time they had a few free moments together. Joe and Paul stood and started their day.

Chapter Two

What If?

"What if . . . ?" Joe was sitting across from Paul while they grabbed a quick lunch in the middle of their daywork. They and Kate had spent the last several hours making sure that the patients under their care were all on the right track to recovery.

"What?" Paul responded.

"I have been thinking about getting a group of us together to talk about our purpose here. Not what we do here at the hospital but what we may be trying to do here in this physical world. What if there is something greater than this here and now?" Joe's hands were in the air as they often were when he finished emotionally expounding on something that he felt deeply about.

"I can see that you have been thinking about this for a while. What is it that you want to explore?" asked Paul.

"Anna has me thinking about the possibilities of something greater than this physical world. What is this life? Is it just a small bit of a greater reality? I would like to have us, as a group, discuss the big questions. What is life's purpose? Is there a soul? That sort of thing." Joe seemed to be pondering other ideas but got up and turned to Paul. "We should get back to the floor and check today's labs."

The afternoon had proceeded uneventfully except for some continued slight worsening of Mr. O'Malley's weakness and a new admission with uncontrolled diabetes. It was approaching 5:00 PM, the end of their daywork, so while Joe had Paul and Kate nearby, he asked, "Can we get together for a bite to eat before things get hopping this evening? I have a few things that I have been thinking about that I thought I would pass by you. Bring Bill along too. I would be curious about any he may have to add."

Bill had been their medical student for the past several weeks and, to Joe, might have some opinions about what he was about to propose. Being a medical student threw one into a unique environment for a couple of months. It was an initial exposure to the various branches of medicine, each with their unique approaches to varied illnesses dealt with in their respective specialties. Through this exposure, the medical student made his decision on which branch to follow to practice for the rest of his productive life. Joe had enjoyed Bill's perspectives on what Joe's crew was accomplishing and felt invested in helping him gain a fulfilling experience from his exposure to this specialty of internal medicine.

The gang gathered in the cafeteria, and once everyone had had a few bites, Joe opened the conversation as he usually did, by making sure that everyone knew their night's responsibilities. "Paul, you have the ICUs, and, Kate, the floor is yours. You keep Bill with you, and let him do whatever you think he can handle. He can see some of the new admits as long as he knows where to find you. I've got the ER covered, and you can call me for problems, consults, whatever. We have Pete's surgical group in the house too if something along their line happens to come up.

"With that said, I thought I would bring up something that I have been thinking about for a while. Let me preface this by stating that this is not at all something that I am requiring of you, but I feel that we may find a discussion interesting, maybe even thought provoking or fulfilling, in a way. We live, through what we do on a daily basis, in the present, in the moment. I want to take a step or two back and ask if there is a deeper purpose, a truer meaning to our existence. This, I think, may have been stimulated in part by my relationship with my present love, Anna. You all know her, and she is, at times, a sounding board for me and a source of stimulating thought when I want to ponder my purpose. To me, she is a deep thinker and a reservoir of spiritual thought or identification. I just think that we could enjoy and maybe benefit by conducting a series of discussions about various topics dealing with the greater universe, that which may be beyond our ability to sense physically but possibly available to us if we decide to investigate critically."

Paul responded, "Joe, I think that that could be interesting, but how would you like to handle these discussions?"

"I think I would start out with us picking one topic each time. Maybe we could meet every few weeks. I feel that, at least to start, I would handle it by choosing one of you to argue in favor of the existence of a certain topic, and someone else would make the argument against it. I would also, for fun, try to possibly have you argue against what I think would be what you would really believe about the topic. For instance, if I had Anna work on a topic like life after death, which we may start with, I would have her take the side against a belief in life after death, because I know that she believes the other way. This will not be a contest to see who wins by swaying the others' thoughts on the subject but by who can make the most acceptable, cogent argument that, the group can say, hits a note of plausibility. And again, by arguing against what you actually believe, I think that the discussions can become more invigorating, even inspiring.

"The chief proponent of either side can include someone to help them out with their arguments and help with supporting background research, which can be cited for support of their premise. I also want to invite Anna and hope she will come and find it interesting enough to participate. Besides the chief participants, once the basic premises are laid out, anyone who comes will be invited to feel free to participate with questions and answers, if they care to add their thoughts or perspectives. I want this to be not only somewhat structured so that we accomplish a good discussion of the intended topic but also an arena for open discussion of anyone's specific viewpoints."

Kate was taking this in. "I think I like this idea. Do you feel that you have enough worked out to get this started?"

"Well, yes, I think we could try it out, if you guys want to." There was a nod of agreement from everyone. "Then why don't we just go ahead and start with the question of life after death. Kate, since you are asking, with your parochial exposure and Catholic upbringing, I want you to argue against life after death. Paul, because I feel that you with your pragmatic approach to things such as a belief in life after death, which, some argue, is a weakness and need for a belief in something more, what Freud even said was a ploy imposed on the peasant masses by their overseers to quell their angst about their plight in life in order to keep them happy and satisfied through a belief in a better future beyond their physical existence, namely, a belief in an afterlife of bliss, I will have you argue in favor of life after death. If I were you, I would consult Anna as I know she can point you toward some good sources.

"Kate, I know that there are many sources in our medical field as well as among other disciplines of science that look toward their answers to this question through solving mysteries scientifically. Use whomever you can find to help your argument. Again, know that each of you probably doesn't hold to a belief in the side of the argument that I am asking you to take, but I think that that will make our discussions more beneficial and exciting."

Everyone seemed interested and, almost in unison, asked, "How do we start this?"

Joe answered, "I'll give you three weeks to prepare, and if you want, we can meet at my place on Friday evening, the eighteenth. I think our schedules are open then. As I said, Anna is going to come also, and any of you can invite a friend along too. Before we meet, though, let me know if you have someone coming so that I can order enough pizza. If our group grows, we will get any newcomers involved too, if they want to. What we will do is, each time we exhaust a topic in one meeting or more, we will pick the next at the end of the meeting. I will try to provide my thoughts on what we accomplished, if anything, during the previous discussion."

With that, dinner finished, their pagers started to awaken requesting a call to the emergency room, and their night on call had begun.

Paul answered his page quickly and, after listening to a new laboratory report, adjusted the medication being delivered by intravenous drip. That done, Joe said his page was from the emergency room and invited Paul to come with him. On arrival there, they were filled in briefly about a patient having difficulty breathing. Evaluation, so far, was showing low blood oxygenation levels, unremarkable findings on chest x-ray, and nonspecific changes on the patient's electrocardiogram. This left a multitude of possibilities, including a blood infection, blood clot in the lungs, early and nonvisible heart attack as yet, or even early pneumonia. It was obvious, though, that the patient was acutely ill and unstable, so an intensive care admission was going to be necessary while they sorted out the cause and treatment over the next hours. They both took a good look at the patient and arranged their treatment plan.

The rest of the evening calmed down with just a few manageable problems, and they were even able to get a couple of hours of sleep before their next day started. By the start of the next day's work, they had signed off the ICU case to the daytime ICU resident service with a probable diagnosis of sepsis due to a kidney infection, and by that afternoon, their time spent with Sub was helpful as usual. The two cases that they presented to him left them with some new ideas on directions to go with the patients. They made it through the rest of the day and went home with catching up on some lost sleep as one of the more pleasant thoughts in each one's mind.

Chapter Three

The First Meeting: Life After Death

The ensuing days went as was usual for their way of life on their unit. Joe heard murmurs and had inklings that Kate and Paul were working on their respective arguments and supporting documents for their meeting coming up soon at Joe's apartment. They both seemed invested in making their case for their side of the discussion.

The time for the meeting came around, and everyone settled in with pizza and drinks. Joe could feel a huddled glow around the room, projecting an anticipation for both the conversation and the aromatic pizza filling the room with welcome comfort. He reasoned that, after all, this was a group of highly motivated, intelligent young adults in training, who rarely had a chance to sit back and enjoy a low-key but stimulating conversation. They were a group of nine—Joe and Anna with Paul, Kate, and Ravi, who had each brought along a friend, and Bill.

After they all had gotten comfortable with something to nibble on and something to wet their lips, Joe opened the conversation with a welcome and his thoughts about what he hoped to accomplish, both socially and intellectually, with these group discussions.

"I am happy to see that we all could make it tonight, and as I mentioned to each of you previously in one way or another, I hope that we find some enjoyment and even some enlightenment with an investigation into what I would consider some of the deeper questions to a purpose, if any, for our life here. More than our pure physical existence and interactions with our encompassing surroundings available to us through our five physical senses, what if anything exists beyond these senses, and are there ways available to us to access this realm?

"And finally, what would the knowledge of this greater existence mean to us, both intellectually and psychically or even spiritually? With that said, I will open this discussion to Paul and Kate, to whom I have assigned the duty or pleasure, as they wish to see it, to argue the existence of life after death. So, guys, go ahead and introduce any assistants whom you may have recruited for this discussion. Paul, since you are going to argue the pro side, you can start with any opening thoughts, and then, Kate, you can put in your opening comments for the con side."

Paul considered rising from his chair but instead cupped his hands in front of him and started, "I have come to believe in, what some may think, my not-so-many years of living in this existence that there may be something beyond. I have been asked here to try to not so much prove that idea but to promote the theory that life or an existence can and will continue after death. Obviously, there can be no proof because to cross over means that one does not come back. We have many stories of people who feel close to death and come back. But have they really seen death?

"What are their stories? We have seen people near death and, at times, after they have been brought back from what many would consider was death. Their heart had stopped for several minutes, or they had had a brain shutdown from a stroke causing acute blood insufficiency. When they came back and became coherent, they related having gone somewhere out of their bodies to a place where they found welcoming former relatives of theirs. These relatives tended to tell them that it was not yet their time to pass but that they had still more to accomplish in the life that they had chosen. My proposal is that there is something beyond the physical body that exists and can be accessed and occasionally remembered—to some more likely to be at a point of acute stress, but to other adepts, that may be available at their request.

"If someone moves out of the body at the time of his death and actually can witness the ado that occurs, I feel that he can, without a sense of pain or other discomfort, watch this with some detachment but also with a sense of completion. 'I am here, and this is it, and now it is my time to move on.' With that opening comment, I will yield to my friendly cocombatant."

Kate stood. "There is not and cannot be any evidence for the possibility of life after death. We have no means to measure what happens or where a persona or—quote, unquote—soul goes after he or she expires. All else is supposition or speculation. Yes, there are stories of those who have come back, but had they actually left? We don't know. Were they just deluded in a possible state of oxygen deprivation?

"I propose that that state is just a place of hypoxic, near-death illusion, which can be explained by brain dysfunction or hallucination at the time of near death. I will yield back."

Following Kate's lead, Paul stood. "So we have drawn the lines. I am frankly enjoying Joe's idea here, and I think that we are going to have fun and maybe get a worthwhile pearl or two from these discussions that we will have tonight and in the future. With that said, I will get back into my proposal that beyond this physical existence, much more exist at many levels, from those related to some of our accessible emotional or mental levels to other purely ethereal or spiritual levels. In the dream state, have you ever been met by someone who, actually, you did not know had passed away, only to find out after that he had, that night, passed on?

"How could that happen? If he has passed, he is dead. What if there is something beyond his physical existence? Could it be a shadow of what he wanted to do before he left? Or could it be that he continues to exist somewhere other than here, actively communicating to us in his way—in our case, through a dream state—to say good-bye?"

Kate responded, "If that is all you have, then I say that dreams are illusions. They are reproductions of pieces of what happened to you over the previous day or two. They are only that and what Freud considered *wish fulfillment*. Do you wish to talk to that person after he was gone? Then he came to you in a fabricated dream to impart a nugget of knowledge that you find revealing."

Joe tentatively raised a hand and, when noticed, spoke. "I just wanted to interject here that with where I see this going, I have decided what our next topic will be. We will discuss it later, either when we reach a break time or when we decide to call it quits for tonight."

Paul then took the floor. "Okay, I'm going to get into it. This is not just an argument about life after death but also really a discussion of the existence of an essence or soul beyond one's purely physical presence. This is what it is that continues beyond death but, if perceived by someone still alive as in the example of the dream visitation, still contains an imprint of the previous physical life to make the visitor recognizable to the one visited.

"Whether we call it a soul or a persisting energy essence, it contains characteristics that are recognizable to the person who is the recipient of the visitation.

"I feel that the hardened disbeliever can ignore the multiple instances of certain people or purported mediums, who seem to have the ability to access an entity who has passed on but can still relay information that only the living relative he is talking to can verify. Sure, there have been charlatans who have exploited people's gullibility at times, but I feel that there are some truly capable and gifted people who can communicate with and receive information from that energy ball or soul that continues to exist beyond the physical form. And I do believe that in a scientifically controlled environment that ability can be investigated and has been confirmed without a doubt."

Kate started, "Paul, I thought you gave up in Missouri, the Show-Me State."

Paul retorted, "Kate, I think I have been shown enough supporting evidence to allow me to accept what I have related."

Continuing, Kate responded, "Well, to me, seeing is believing. Without personal experience, I am unwilling to accept what other people say is a given to them. I guess I am the Missourian here.

"Then, too, that leaves me with that belief of something existing beyond physical death as wishful thinking. One of the great tenets of religion is the existence of life after death, which, again, referring to Freud's supposition, is just a ruse to keep the less advantaged hoi polloi in line with a promise of a greater reward if they stay in line and be good while they are alive."

Deciding to move to a different perspective, Paul began, "Assuming there is an existence after death, what may it be? What is involved in it? Does the entity continue on as he did here, gaining more experience and knowledge with a widened perspective once released from his confinements of physicality? Or does he/she/it fly off on a tangent from where he broke away from his circle of physical life existence?"

Joe broke in, saying, "I am enjoying this so far, but I think that this sounds like a good place to break for something to eat, and then we can see where Paul plans to take this."

Everyone agreed, and they began getting up, a couple at a time, to grab a piece or two of pizza and something to drink. Joe could tell, as they settled back and started eating, that from the small conversations, everyone seemed to be enjoying the discussion so far, and a few seemed to be working on ideas that they may want to interject into the argument.

After a little while, everyone seemed more relaxed and had quieted down, so Paul started once more, continuing with his train of thought. "I believe that this soul/essence, which I will call 'he' for simplicity's sake while still meaning 'she or it' also, once detached from his physicality, continues on with choices concerning what he can do. He can choose to hang around the physical locale and the other people that he was familiar with. But he can also choose to explore his new environment to better understand his new limits and the rules that apply to his new condition. In his new situation, he can continue to learn more things that can further his development to a goal, which, I feel, is beyond the confines of our present argument tonight. Perhaps that goal could be a point of discussion on another night." With that, Paul paused.

Joe raised a hand and, when recognized by Paul, remarked, "So you are suggesting that this entity's physical existence is not the end-all of his totality but, instead, just a part of his overall experience?"

Paul nodded and responded, "Yes, I am saying that his physical existence is just a part of his complete, greater existence. I will go one step further and even suggest that his physical existence was a conscious choice and that there are some entities or souls who may opt never to participate in a physical existence at all. I propose that an earthly existence is just one of many options to choose from, but it has unique experiences available only if the earthly life is selected to be experienced."

Bill raised his hand, and when Paul nodded, he spoke. "You talk about a period of nonphysical growth or education. I was raised as a non-Catholic Christian in a Lutheran or Protestant environment. We were taught that after death, our life is evaluated in our presence by Peter, and a decision is made to be allowed ascension into heaven or to be condemned to hell or to be sent to purgatory for an additional period of time based on the life we lived. There are other beliefs in some Christian factions where there is a more literal translation of the Bible in which after death, the soul remains buried with the physical body until Jesus's second coming when he decides a disposition regarding a person's life in order to send the soul to one of those three places for eternity."

Paul answered, "Yes, there are some people who believe that which are based on literal interpretations of passages in Revelation, but my investigations in researching for tonight led me more toward accepting more varied choice of options for the soul freed of its physical bonds. And again, stories of the adepts who can leave their physical bodies to explore nonphysical realms and return back to their physical body and their life seem to support the extra, available choices."

Kate jumped up. "Okay, before we completely fall off the deep end here, I want to remind all of us that this is purely unsubstantiated fiction. Those who have died cannot confirm their continued experiences to us, and those who say they fly around at night are hallucinating. Tell my grandmother to visit me while I am awake, and tell me that she saw what I did yesterday. Then I could entertain the possibility somewhat of this having a chance of being true or real."

Bill raised a hand and was given the floor. "Paul, you mentioned a couple of different things that the soul can choose to do, from hanging around and watching his living relatives to exploring avenues of further learning. Can you tell us more about the various possible options open to the soul in this state?"

Responding, Paul said, "Sure. I have run across descriptions of many different options open to the soul or entity in this state. One I mentioned already is to stay around those he was with during his physical life and, from his greater perspective, influence those people in making some of their important choices in their life, such as encouraging them to check on subtle signs or cluing them to possible downturns in their health before it is too late.

"Other options could include visiting a grand university in their realm where they could further their knowledge in a field of interest that they held in their previous life. A former doctor or nurse—in deference to Anna, our nurse representative in the group tonight—they could study medicine at a more psychic level and again apply it in interacting with the physical entities still here participating in earthly existence. These communications could come through in dreams or spontaneous revelations or aha moments.

"Also, the great hall of inventions could be accessed and used to help an inventor looking for a solution to a perplexing problem, allowing him to invent a solution.

"There are many possibilities. Another would be just to explore, at this more open level, any questions that the entity may have had during his physical life just to gain a wider, greater understanding for himself."

Ravi raised a hand, and Paul responded, saying, "Let's hear from our distinguished surgical colleague."

Ravi started, "I was raised in a household observing some Hindu traditions with its hierarchy of various gods who interacted with each other and attempted some controlling interactions with the physical beings here on earth. I ended up tending to look for my answers to the difficult questions in science and grew to consider a belief in all these ethereal beings as a colloquialism of beliefs in my society. I agree with that, though science cannot yet provide us with the ultimate answers to questions like this. It is the path that I decided to take as a scientist."

Kate added, stating, "Absent a truly verifiable visitation from a departed person, I have no choice but to agree with Ravi that, without seeing truly undisputable evidence of contact with a dead person's remaining essence or whatever one chooses to call it, we have no proof."

Joe jumped in to say, "I have to relate, though, that there are instances of highly intelligent, pure scientists, who, when they reach their limits of where their sciences can take them and they see the great complexity beyond, can have a revelatory moment wherein they suddenly awaken to a strong possibility of a Supreme Being's hands in the works."

Kate retorted, "I think, much more often, they just sit there stumped and feel that maybe tomorrow, an answer will present itself, and they will then be able to move on. Possibly, those with the moment of revelation have just given up and feel inadequate at not being able to move forward."

Joe stood up and started, "If anyone has anything more to ask or add, raise a hand." When no one did, he continued, "It is getting late, and I think we can stop here. I just want to say that I have enjoyed our get-together tonight. We did not solve anything. No one won, but that was not the purpose. Instead, the discussion itself was the purpose, and by doing this, I hope we can all look at this question of life after death more critically.

"With that said, I want to propose our topic for our next gathering in about a month, and I want to continue along these lines by considering the question of reincarnation and how different religions deal with that idea. Being Catholic, I would like to take a side myself and go against the Catholic belief, arguing in favor, and, Ravi, though you are Hindu, I am sure that you have had many discussions with Buddhist friends of yours growing up in India. So I would like you to argue against."

Looking at Anna, he added, "I will tell you now that I will be using Anna's help in my research and discussion as well. So for now, let's disband and plan on getting together in about four weeks when we can find a time convenient for us all. Again, anyone else is welcome to come to these discussions, if any of you find someone asking."

With that, they all got up, put on their jackets, said good night to Joe and to one another, and filed out of the door and into the cool night air.

Chapter Four

Back on the Floor

The next morning began just like any other. Once everyone gathered and they were caught up on any happenings that occurred since they left at the end of the day yesterday, they began making their rounds, visiting with the patients one by one as they went methodically down the hall. With each stop, they reviewed the chart, discussed the plan of care with the patient, and made formal plans with orders to be carried out to continue or adjust treatment or to further search diagnostically where needed if the actual cause of illness was not yet fully understood.

Mrs. Hendricks, with the leg infection, seemed to be responding well to the chosen antibiotic regimen. She had only a low-grade fever now and was feeling better. Her elevated white blood cell count, originally raised by the infection, had been showing a drop toward normal.

Mr. O'Malley was continuing to become weaker and seemed to be losing some sensation to touch over his lower abdomen. They decided to call in a consultation with the pulmonary service, in case his breathing started to become labored, and a consult with the hematology service to discuss whether it could be helpful to start a plasma exchange in an attempt to remove detrimental antibodies, which could be attacking his nervous system.

Though Sally's stroke had stabilized, the laboratory test results that they were waiting for were not yet available. Joe made it Bill's job to go down to the hematology lab to see if he could prod the staff there to expedite the completion of the tests. Sometimes, showing a little more urgency could motivate the lab personnel to take some special attention to getting results available. Joe remembered and sometimes followed his high school biology teacher's favorite saying, "The noisiest wheel gets the most oil."

Once the more urgent duties were taken care of, the four of them had a chance to sit for a few minutes and plan their day's work. Joe asked Paul to make a call to the residents working with the subspecialty physicians in both pulmonary medicine and hematology to be sure that they could get their requested consults underway as soon as they could. He assigned Bill to look into the effect of plasmapheresis or plasma exchange in patients with ascending myelitis or Guillain-Barré syndrome as he suspected Mr. O'Malley to be suffering from. This was more for Bill's edification than anything else, but he felt it wouldn't hurt to have Bill talk about it to the others for a few minutes just to review the current ideas about its theoretical application and efficacy.

With their assignments made, Paul and Bill set off on their tasks with plans for them all to meet before lunch to discuss end results from their forays. Joe decided to spend a little extra time on some questions he had about a few of their patients' enigmas or unclear findings as yet. Kate decided to tag along and to provide any insights she may have or to, at least, be a sounding board for Joe.

Once lunchtime arrived, they were all back together and decided to grab something from the cafeteria so that they could bring it to a meeting room where they could relax and let Bill have his few minutes to present the information that he had researched about ascending myelitis and autoantibodies as they could relate to Mr. O'Malley's condition. Bill also checked in with the hematology lab and relayed that they promised to have some results on Sally's blood-clotting studies by the end of the day.

Chapter Five

The Second Meeting: Reincarnation

A few days later, while Joe was chatting with Mary, she mentioned that she had heard about the meeting he had with his crew and friends. She said that she was interested, and when Joe invited her to come to the next one, she accepted. Joe felt sure that there would be no problems with either Anna or Mary if they were both there, and when asked, both said that they were perfectly comfortable being together. Joe told Mary also to be prepared to enjoy herself and to certainly feel free to enter the discussion as the spirit moved her.

Over the next few weeks, each day came and went with some days easy, and more often, at least one surprise presented itself. Joe felt to himself that those surprises were just to keep them on their toes and to keep them interested. During the period, Mrs. Hendricks' leg infection improved, and she was sent home with oral antibiotics and orders for home health nurse visits to tend her wound and to monitor her recovery. Mr. O'Malley seemed to be responding to the plasma exchange and was felt, after a while, to be ready for transfer to a nursing rehabilitation center to help him gain his strength before being safe to go home. Finally, Sally was found to be suffering from a predisposition for excessive blood clotting, so she was started on medication to counteract that, and she was slowly improving with inpatient physical therapy.

The evening of the fifteenth came around, and everyone—including the new attendee, Mary—began to show up at Joe's apartment again for another night of anticipated, lively, and enlightening talk.

Once again, after everyone was settled in and comfortable, Joe opened, saying, "I am glad that we are able to be back again and that we can welcome a new participant, Mary, who has joined us. Tonight, we are going to try to critically consider the question of reincarnation. I have decided to argue the case in favor while I have asked Ravi to argue against. With the sides chosen, I will yield to Ravi to open the discussion with any beginning remarks he wishes to make."

Ravi took the cue and stood. "With that said, I will start by saying, as Kate in our first meeting, that the existence of reincarnation is going to be hard to prove to the skeptic. Despite numerous anecdotes, which I am sure Joe will apprise us of, I am going to let Joe get into some of his specific points of argument so that I know what I need to disprove or cast doubt on. I am going to give the floor to Joe." Ravi nodded toward Joe and seated himself.

Joe arose, starting, "I am going to remark on several different instances chronicled about some long-held beliefs and many reports from the nineteenth and twentieth centuries, several in the last few decades. There actually have been suggestions that as we were nearing the end of the century recently, there was a growing interest in spiritual studies. It is reported that the same has seemed to occur in the previous century, and again, this has been suggested to be a common recurring theme often as other centuries neared their completion. I did not, however, hear of anyone suggesting a reason for that phenomenon, only just an observation of the occurrence."

Joe continued, "I will give a couple of reported examples and then let Ravi respond before I go further. I will mention, at the start here, that looked at purely scientifically, it will be impossible to prove without a doubt that reincarnation exists, but again, that is not our purpose here. I do, however, plan tonight to give several compelling examples, which make a strong argument for the possibility and even the probability of the greater reality that our present physical lives are not the only ones that our nonphysical center of being experiences. Just out of common sense, think about the complexity of this physical world and its offerings throughout time. Why would we experience such a little part of the whole available here with just one trip when there would be so much more that we learn if we had multiple go-arounds? It has been stated that in early Christianity, there was a belief in reincarnation, but in the first couple of centuries after Christ, it was removed from the Scripture and the system of beliefs that Christianity followed as truths, because it was deemed by those in charge to be a problem for the control of the masses. What if reincarnation was promoted as a truth? The priests then worried that a person could decide that he need not follow all the rules to find reward in heaven because he could worry about being pious and do all the things a good Christian should do on his next time around. So all mention of reincarnation was wiped out of the Scriptures and never brought up for a topic of liturgical discussion."

Joe stopped for a sip of soda and then went on. "It has been found by anthropologists studying many old aboriginal societies, which have not had much contact with the Western culture or our industrialized society, which has tended to push the individual away from nature, that there frequently tends to be a matter-of-fact belief in reincarnation. The Inuit people of the region we call Alaska have such a strong belief that when someone dies, his belongings are kept aside until a young child can describe the belongings and their purposes to the tribe. The child is then regarded as the reincarnated soul of the owner of those trinkets and is given repossession of that property. It is interesting too that the religion is ancient in this society as in the religion of aboriginal groups from Central America, Russia, Africa, and even our North American Indian tribes and elsewhere. Its common thread is called shamanism, and we may discuss more about these beliefs at another meeting as we get into other topics.

"There is much more to go, but I will take a break and grab a piece of pizza. As an aside, maybe we will have something different to eat next time. Perhaps I can get us some tapas bites just to change our menu. I am going to give Ravi a chance for anything he wishes to argue while I take a few bites." With that, he picked a piece to eat and sat back down next to Anna.

Ravi rose slowly but with a slight smirk on his face and began, "I am going to start with a generalization here and then see if I can respond to some of Joe's specific points. When a blade of grass dies, does it contemplate its life of freedom in a poorly groomed field or look for meaning in its tortured life of weekly dismemberment by that loud machine ridden on or pushed by that biped animal while it is cut by a sharp blade? What possible purpose could be served from its perspective from its repeated anguish?

"If we are going to talk about reincarnation, we are going to have to include karma to give reincarnation a reason for existence. Karma, or tit for tat, would serve as a keel to point that reincarnating soul down its optimal path toward its supposed goal. Does everything on this planet, from the amoeba to the most complex organism, reincarnate to reach its greatest or highest spiritual potential attainable in this physical laboratory or realm? Or are we, as human beings, the only physical organisms with spirit attached that undergo multiple rebirths?

"Were we once a blade of grass, which now, through rebirths, made it to the supposed optimal physical being, which is the only physical organism capable of ultimately bringing its carry-on soul to a point of release from the cycle of rebirth or jail imposed on the spirits inhabiting this physical world and allowing attainment of enlightenment in traditional Buddhism or the state of satori in Zen Buddhism? Another possibility is that the soul found this world and the human animal compatible with its soul enough to be able to enter it to experience the physical world.

"Or is this a manufactured joke perpetrated on the masses for whatever reasons the initiator or Supreme Being has. Again, as mentioned at our first discussion, reasons could be, according to Freud, to give the weak individual a meaning or purpose in his life other than to just live it or, according to Marx, to keep the rabble-rousing by the hoi polloi at a minimum through giving them a belief in later-realized rewards.

"So reincarnation, as a concept created in the context of and given a home in some organized religions and even developed in early societies, is actually not much different from a view in Christianity with the belief in a need for one perfectly lived Christian life necessary for the later ultimate reward. Both are looking to give the person a reason to live a well-intentioned life for reward in the future. It is just that the Christian is to do it with his one life while the reincarnation believer needs to do it over several times to reach his final ultimate reward.

"Or, again, is it just hogwash created by some to control everyone else so that the few in places of authority can rule the many? Let's see where else Joe plans to take us." Ravi turned to Joe, nodded, and went for more to drink before sitting down.

Joe rose, asking, "Before I move on, does anyone have anything they wish to comment on?"

No hands being raised, Joe began. "Let's move on and ask the question, 'if reincarnation exists, does it serve a purpose, and if so, what is that purpose?' Possibly, reasoning out a purpose can give it some credibility for its existence. We have already stated that the cycle of rebirths gives the soul multiple chances to progress forward to an ultimate goal, one of which will be the continuing cycle of rebirths. That, in a way, I would consider the ultimate in circular reasoning." He got a slight chuckle from the group.

"What happens once that goal is reached? Buddhists believe in that state of enlightenment or satori as Ravi kindly mentioned. It is a state of bliss and, seemingly, an end-all. But then what? Bliss forever, for me, could start to get boring. There are other nonsecular views that attainment of that state is merely a completion of one stage along a longer path. It means that all the lessons that the spirit has to gain from this physical realm have been acquired, so it is time to move onto a new stage for new lessons with the ultimate goal possibly being a completeness that is possibly equivalent to a state of all knowingness or godliness or possibly returning to be with God or the source.

"It has been suggested that this physical journey is just one of many options, which the soul has to choose from. It is felt, though, that if the soul opts for this learning experience, he ends up at the end of his journey fuller and more well-rounded than if he skipped this somewhat difficult task called earth experience.

"Also, it has been posited that once the choice is made to the physical earth experience, the soul becomes trapped in the cycle of rebirths until the complete lesson or knowledge to be gained by the earth experience is attained. Once the final attainment is reached, the soul has finished his schooling here, ends his rebirth cycle, and moves on with what he has gained.

"Along with this repeated rebirth, the interim period is a time to reflect on his previous physical existence with the ability to make choices for lessons to be learned in the next go-around on earth, and situations are set up to place him in positions that allow the physically incarnated soul to confront those lessons.

"I am sure you have noticed that I do not think that the end of the cycle of physical rebirths is the end of the journey wherever that is going. I feel that it is just a completed stage of a bigger path. But tonight, where that path leads after the physical rebirth cycle is completed is beyond our topic of discussion. Maybe we can discuss some other parts of the longer trek at another time."

Anna raised a hand, and when Joe nodded her way, she said, "I just wanted to mention a little about possibilities in those other stages along the greater path. They could be a totally different physical environment with similar lessons or explorations more into the emotional level of our being for greater understanding of its potentials. Or it could investigate a more mental layer of our existence. Each of these levels could come with different attributes or tools useful in the exploration of these environments, much like we have physical touch, sight, hearing, and smell to help us evaluate and interact with our physical world." Anna gestured with her hand back toward Joe.

Joe asked, "Are there any other questions or thoughts?"

Paul raised a hand and, when recognized, asked, "You made passing remarks about those in charge who decided to remove reincarnation from the mainstream thought of Christianity because of the fears that the people may, with that knowledge of rebirth, decide to say, 'Let's blow off this being good thing this time around and have some fun because we can just make up for it next time'?"

Joe asked Anna if she wanted to respond, and she eagerly stood. "That problem was addressed by the Buddhist priests by stating that to be human was a gift and to squander that would cause a drop back further away from the ultimate goal of enlightenment, and that entity that had a human incarnation may find himself back in a lower animal life form with several more incarnations needed to get back to where he fell from. So to be human carried with it a responsibility to be good. This thought has even been taken so far as to say that to be human and to be exposed to Buddhist thought and not take it to heart was a loss because following the Buddhist path was the quickest way to satori or enlightenment.

"Not that I am going to take it that far because that tends to be a common thread in many religions. A Catholic is taught that to not be a Catholic is a waste of one's life because only a true Catholic can get to heaven. That was a cause of the great Reformation or breakaway from that 'mine is the only way' mentality, which, I believe, is self-defeating because a 'my religion is the only way' thought flies against a system of tolerance, which is of greater spiritual worth than that of intolerance. In fact, that intolerance has been the cause of many of our great wars of history and now. I will end here before I go too far into a diatribe."

Anna sat back down, and Joe asked, "Any other questions?"

Bill raised a hand, and when Joe nodded, he stood, saying, "If everyone reincarnates repeatedly, why are there only a few anecdotes available relating people's stories?"

Joe responded, "I have wondered that myself, but my reading suggested an answer. In order for reincarnation to serve its purpose, its existence must be hidden from those of us living our present lives. Only with the ignorance about our previous existence can we exercise the option of free choice, which is necessary for our spiritual growth. If we knew of our previous lives and our plan for the present life, we could not have free choice because we would just be playing a role concocted before we got here, and we would have no ability to gain from the experience. The previous lives are available to us and help us in our decision making for our next life when we do a life review between lives to see what we gained or missed on our last earth foray and decide what we want to confront in the next one. That, I think, is why we can't access any earlier life experiences while here this time. I hope that gives you a possible answer to your question."

With no more hands raised, Joe said, "I have discussed some possible sightings of reincarnation in my early remarks and then discussed some views on the purpose of reincarnation, so I think I will end here and give the discussion back to Ravi."

Ravi rose and began, "Yes, we have just anecdotes. That story from the mid last century of an American woman remembering a past life in, I think, Ireland could have been developed through suggestion and finding a few possible connections in the investigation. Maybe the woman heard stories when she was younger that she internalized, believing that they were her previous self in an earlier life.

"Then, too, the Inuits—they had such small closed communities that there may have been stories of their fathers or uncles that were likely commonly told to pass a cold winter's night. They, again, could have heard enough and internalized it only to repeat it, convincing relatives that they were the true incarnations of former relatives.

"The only way we are going to know is after we have passed on, and for purposes of this discussion, that will be the only proof, and to stick it in your craw, once we know, as Joe related, we can't bring that knowledge back with us consciously the next time around.

"I am done here, so if this discussion has been sufficiently exhausted, I suggest we end it here."

Joe, standing up, agreed and then said, "Before we go, I want to suggest our next topic, which will be a bit of a change from these first two. I want to look into the concept of linear versus nonlinear time. Since this is a bit different, I will take volunteers. Think about it, discuss it, and let me know tomorrow who will be in charge of each side of the argument."

Everyone stood up, stretched, and those few who were still hungry grabbed the last few pieces of cold pizza and finished them off. Then with coats donned, they all shook hands, thanked Joe for the enjoyable evening, and went on their way.

Chapter Six

A New Day and Night

The next morning started quietly. Joe had a chance to catch Mary and hand her a cup of hot tea before she went in for her change-of-shift meeting of nurses. She had only an hour or so from the end of the talk at Joe's until she had to go to the hospital to do her night shift, so she looked a little tired. Joe had been glad that she attended the discussion the night before, and she thanked him for the invitation.

It was just before seven, and Joe found Kate, Paul, and Bill together on the floor and joined them. They were just a few minutes into organizing their day when a nurse's aide, who was helping to watch the floor while the nurses were in their meeting, came up to them. "I am sorry to interrupt you," she said, "but a new admission came in a few hours ago with a fever and is getting more short of breath, and her blood pressure has dropped twenty points in the past fifteen minutes. Could you take a look at her for me, please?"

Joe dispatched Kate to take a look. A couple of minutes later, she came out into the hall and yelled for Joe and told the aide to dial the operator and have her call for a respiratory arrest code, stating that she felt it was imminent.

Joe came rushing, passing the aide running the other way to the unit secretary to get her on the phone to the operator to ask her to broadcast the code. Kate had already opened the IV, trying to help the tanking blood pressure, but the patient was visibly in respiratory distress. The lungs sounded fine on quick exam, and Joe asked Kate, "What do you know about this patient?"

Kate responded, "I was told by Jim, the second-year resident on call last night, that she came in a few hours ago with some abdominal pain and a low-grade fever. She was pancultured and started on empiric antibiotics."

The patient, whose name was as yet unknown to Joe, looked to be in her fifties. Joe took a quick look at her abdomen, and what had been reported to Kate as mild left lower quadrant tenderness had now progressed to a completely rock-hard abdomen. Joe, looking at Kate, said, "We have a surgical abdomen here, either a perforated diverticulum or, worse, a ruptured colon due to a colon tumor. We need a surgical consult now. Call Pete from the surgical service on call today, and get him over here stat. Get some anaerobic coverage with the antibiotics too. Once you get those things done, call the attending to let him know what is going on, and ask him which attending surgeon he wants called in."

He then turned to the nurse's aide and said, "Linda, go find the day-shift nurse who has this patient, and get her out here to get these new orders implemented. Have her find me when Pete gets here too." He left the room to tell the other guys to start rounds without him, saying that he would join them once the situation here was under control.

From there, things seemed to calm down and move fairly smoothly. Pete had gotten there quickly, evaluated the patient, who was now known as fifty-four-year-old Mrs. Steiner, and agreed with Joe that they were dealing with a perforated colon for whatever reason to be determined when they opened her up and got into her abdomen. He called the operating room to get an emergency surgery scheduled, called his attending, and had the nurse inform Mrs. Steiner's husband that she was on her way to surgery. He then ordered some vasopressors to try to stabilize her blood pressure.

Joe, finding everything under control in Pete's capable hands, left to see how his crew was doing and to join them for what he hoped would be an otherwise quiet day, because he was feeling a little tired too, being unable to fall asleep the night before due to his ruminations about the discussion that they had.

Then, too, while making his way to Paul and the others, he thought about his upcoming evening. He and Anna had agreed to go out to one of their favorite Italian restaurants. He knew he was in a rut, enjoying the linguini with assorted shellfish, but those clams, mussels, and scallops, along with calamari in a marinara sauce, looked, smelled, and tasted good every time he had it. Maybe someday, he would try something else (Anna seemed to usually enjoy the ravioli), but wasn't it okay also to pick a restaurant based on the meal that one knows the restaurant does well with? Since he was a bit tired too and his crew was on call again tomorrow, he had plans not too be out very late.

He met up with the others, and they filled him in on the patients that they had already seen to catch him up on what they had done already, and then they continued together down the hallway to complete their rounds.

There was another new case of anemia in a middle-aged man. The cause was as yet undetermined with some labs still pending from his early morning blood draws. They decided to have Kate present whatever they had on him to Sub when they had teaching rounds again in the afternoon.

The rest of their rounds went smoothly, and they had a little time before lunch. Kate used that time to run off to see what she could retrieve from the hematology lab, regarding their new patient's anemia, before they met for a quick bite, because they were going to meet with Sub right after lunch.

The teaching rounds did end up being fairly interesting because the cause of the anemia was still undetermined. Sub had some suggestions including a bone marrow biopsy to look for nutrient supplies and any sign of an infiltrative disease. While Sub usually did or supervised those biopsies with most residents, he had watched Joe do enough of them that he was comfortable with just telling Joe to call the hematology lab to come up and help with the procedure and the handling of the specimen once Joe procured it. The group also discussed a couple of other cases with diagnostic and treatment puzzles, getting some good suggestions in return.

The rest of the afternoon was fairly uneventful, and they were able to finish by five. Joe got home and cleaned up both himself and some of the leftover mess from the night before to make the place presentable for Anna later. Then he drove to pick up Anna from her job. She was working as a research biologist studying the effects of selected advantageous traits added to agricultural crops for greater disease resistance along with better productivity and nutritive value. She had gotten her undergraduate training in downstate Illinois and was trying to continue some advanced education toward a postgraduate degree while she worked. She felt her work was going to be useful for expanding population struggles worldwide. The nature of her work, like Joe's, caused her to work seven days a week even if Sundays were just a quick visit to check on her specimens. Joe enjoyed it when she discussed her work with an obvious passion, and he knew that she felt the same way about his work. They both were helping people but on different levels, her work helping at a group or population level while his was at a more personal level.

Joe had had a few relationships before Anna, enough to know that she was the one that he hoped to be his last and lifelong one. He felt comfortable in his belief that she saw the two of them the same way. He just seemed to enjoy her company and conversation and was sure that whatever came their way in the future, they would be able to handle it just fine together.

He arrived at her work, and as he started walking to her building, she was already coming out because she was watching for him. They greeted each other with a warm hug and kiss. Anna put her jacket on, and they walked to his car for their trip to the restaurant. Once they were seated there, had ordered their meals, and had taken a sip of their drinks, they caught each other up on their day. Anna was feeling energized with a promising new breakthrough on one of her research projects. More time would tell, but she thought a new strain of maize may have at least a 10 percent increase in yield. Joe loved it when she talked about her work with passion. He knew that feeling because he felt the same way about his work often, and to him, it was a perk that not everyone was able to experience.

Joe had been ruminating about the future also and changed the subject. "Anna, I have been thinking that if Sub can help me get a fellowship with his mentor in Houston next July, I think we should seriously think about a June wedding, and then we can go down there together."

Anna, without hesitation, said, "Well, Joe, I have been thinking about that too. They have a good program in my field down there also, so I am sure I can find some work. I have been talking to my sister, Marilyn, about getting started with wedding plans once we set a date."

Joe replied, "Let's look at early June because I could probably finagle a week off if we don't go too late into the month, because I will need to be back at work for the end of June with the shift into the new resident year on July 1."

Anna answered, "Sounds like a good plan to me."

Their dinners were served, and they got to eating, sharing occasionally as they often did. They chatted about little things—the weather, the upcoming winter, his mother's upcoming birthday—and then once dinner was done and Joe paid the bill, they left to take Joe's car back to his apartment for a movie and some quiet time together.

Anna relaxed on the couch while Joe brewed some hot tea for them to relax with. Once that was ready, he settled next to Anna, offering her a mug, and they found a movie that they could agree on. After that was started, they gave each other a kiss and cuddled up as they watched television. Joe enjoyed these quiet times together, being close, and looked forward with anticipation to many years of these special moments.

Once the movie concluded, they caught a little of the local news and weather before heading off to bed. He relished the moments as they helped each other with removing their clothes. The sight of her partially naked body as they disrobed and the touch of her skin as well as her aroma both calmed him with comfort and excited him with anticipation. They slipped under the covers and embraced, kissing lovingly. Her caresses and purrs as he moved his hands over her body brought tingles over his entire being, and as they enjoyed their peak together, he felt complete and a part of their oneness together. He then sank back, spent and completely at one with the universe. Still embraced, they then drifted off to a restful sleep.

Chapter Seven

The Third Meeting: Time

Joe's day went fairly easily. Their night on call was average with three new admissions, one being a middle-aged woman with upper gastrointestinal bleeding. Joe was putting his bet on a duodenal ulcer as the cause, but they would find out more once she underwent endoscopy later that morning, now that she seemed stable. It was interesting that it had been found that duodenal ulcers were more common in the spring and fall, theories being income taxes in the spring and family changes in the fall with the onset of school and worries about upcoming holidays. More recently, once a bacterium was shown often to be the cause, it was felt that the life cycle of that organism could explain some of the swing in ulcer incidences throughout the year.

Pete and Bill stopped by to see Joe in the afternoon to say that the meeting group had agreed on the main participants for the discussion on "time" at their next meeting. Pete said that he had heard of their previous meeting and wanted to join in and what better way than to take a side of the argument. He wanted to argue for nonlinear time while Bill would take the other side. Joe liked the choices and wished them good luck with working up their cases. He also told them he had many thoughts about this, and they were welcome to use him as a sounding board or for references to look into.

The next few weeks continued smoothly, and the time to meet was upon them. Joe had catered some tapas finger foods with chips and salsa and made some sangria for anyone who wanted more than just soda or water.

Once the night for the meeting came, everyone began to arrive around seven at Joe's apartment, and as they entered, he gestured toward a table with food and drinks. He said, "I have ordered out for several different tapas bites, some with beef, pork, or chicken along with some Spanish rice. I also made some red wine sangria if you want it, or choose any soda, or make your own mixed 'poisons' as you wish."

After everyone had a bite to eat and a beverage, they settled in and got comfortable. They all seemed relaxed and ready to get started, so Joe stood holding Anna's hand. He said, "Before I introduce our combatants tonight, I just wanted to announce that Anna and I have set a date for a wedding, the second Saturday in June. We hope that all of you will be there to help us celebrate." There followed some clapping, cheer, and congratulations with smiles all around.

Joe then continued, "Tonight, we are going to investigate one of my favorite ruminations, that of the nature of time. Bill is going to argue for linear time while Pete, our new member tonight, is going to take the case for time being nonlinear. I am going to enjoy this as I hope we all will. With that said, I will give the floor to Bill so that we can get started."

Once Joe sat, Bill rose and began, "Pete and I have worked on this together, so we both know a little about each other's arguments though I hope to still have a couple of surprises for him.

"I will start with the obvious. Time is linear. We all know that what we experienced yesterday was yesterday. It is behind us and gone. We don't know what tomorrow will bring because it won't happen until tomorrow. Imagine the chaos it would bring if we could experience or foretell tomorrow today, before tomorrow happens. We could win the lottery every time, but that doesn't happen, because the lottery numbers for tomorrow haven't been drawn live on television yet.

"Another problem would occur also if time were not linear. That would mean that the future is fixed, and if that is the case, we are just acting out a role already set in stone. If we were going to be in a particular place a day away from here tomorrow, we would be getting now to get there. No matter what our motivations are at this moment, we would be making the move to be there when we are supposed to be there, and we would be leaving now. That sounds like even if we thought we had free will, we are just playing a role that has been predetermined. We have then lost that free choice that we talked about last time. So the future can't be there yet without our loss of free will.

"Now that I have laid out a few ideas, I will give the floor to Pete so that we can see how he can get around these ideas." With that, Bill gestured toward Pete and sat down after getting a couple of tapas and refilling his glass.

Pete stood and, with a nod toward Bill, began, "I will agree with most of what Bill has said. The problem is in the perspective that we are coming from or using. In this physical world, we have agreed to use the convention of linear time. Here, it is the only way to make sense of our existence as Bill has clearly pointed out.

"But if we look at time from the focus of a different nonphysical plane, we can see much more. I am going to use our reference to nonphysical levels or planes of existence mentioned by Anna in your previous discussion. Sure, if we view time from only this physical level that occupies our main awareness, time has to be linear or the construct of our world would fall apart completely. But if we move to higher levels or planes to which Anna has made reference, we first meet the astral plane. Actually, there, the same rules of linear time still seem to exist. Cause and effect still exist at the astral level, but we will see, as we go farther up the planes, that they happen to disconnect. At the astral level, it is really the spatial conventions of the physical plane that tend to break down. Linear time still holds together, though.

"It takes moving to higher planes of existence, really to a point that our physical nature or being has dissolved and becomes a nonplayer, to find a place where linear time also melts away. At this level, all that was, is, or will be exist as one and can be accessed at will. Here, time is nonlinear.

"To remedy Bill's conundrum about the lottery numbers, it is suggested by the Buddhist religion, and I am sorry to have to bring religion into this otherwise secular discussion and plan to do it only rarely, that it still is not possible to find tomorrow's lottery numbers in this state, because such self-aggrandizement is not possible because of the injury that would be done to the receiver-of-the-information's karma or spiritual assets. Frankly, it is not beneficial and can be detrimental to use one's higher psychic energies for personal physical world gain, so except for an occasional possible slip causing a brief view of tomorrow's lottery numbers, it does not help and is of no interest for the higher self to dwell on such a thing. If those lottery numbers became visible, it would be more because of a spontaneous mistake or a breach in the time continuum than by anyone's efforts to see them."

Pete continued after a sip from his glass. "I want to change direction here and develop a model that we can use to show this movement through time, which would be possible if time, or the past and future, all existed at once with our present, thus defining nonlinear time. Once we have created this model, we will use it to visit tomorrow's lottery numbers again.

"Time is considered the fourth dimension while the first three are purely spatial. I will give you each a piece of paper and lay it in front of you. What lies along the edge, moving from left to right, represents a spatial plane's left-to-right axis, and the edge moving away from you represents forward and backward. Now we have anywhere on a spatial plane represented on the surface of the paper. To get the third dimension, flip that paper so that it stands vertically, and consider everything on that spatial plane or two dimensions to be represented by the top edge of the paper. Draw an imaginary line perpendicular to that edge, and that line represents up-and-down, the third dimension. Once you turn that paper horizontally again, the two dimensions, left-and-right and forward-and-backward, are on the line going left to right in front of you, and the edge moving away from you becomes up-and-down. We now have three dimensions represented on a two-dimensional piece of paper.

"Now take this one step further by again turning the paper vertically, and now we have all three spatial dimensions—right-and-left, forward-and-backward, and up-and-down-represented by that line along the top edge. Again, draw an imaginary line perpendicular to that edge, and we now can represent time, the fourth dimension. Turn that paper flat on your desk again, and you have all three spatial dimensions on the horizontal or x-axis and time along the vertical y-axis. We can now see everywhere we move spatially through time on this two-dimensional sheet of paper. A dot in a specific location represents where you are in space and time. Your life spans from the bottom of the paper at y-axis zero point or left corner at the bottom to the top left corner, and where you go spans left to right.

"With this representation, we can see our life starting at point 0, 0 at the lower left corner of the paper, moving as a line moving to the right through space and up the paper through time to the end of your life somewhere along the right edge of the paper. Life becomes a traverse across the paper from jumping on at 0, 0 at birth and hopping off somewhere along the right edge.

"Then, reincarnation becomes a move from one paper to another, and what you have briefly alluded to in the last discussion—such things as life review, choices made about the next life, or other nonphysical ventures—happen in the space between the two separate pieces of paper."

Pete asked, "Is everyone comfortable with this so far? I want to be sure that we are clear on this part before I move on."

Joe raised a hand, and seeing Pete's nod, he interjected, "At another meeting, I think we will probably take a more in-depth look at the multitude of options open to the entity during this time in this so-called in-between state, which is actually not just a depot to sit and wait for the next train or next life but instead is also open to many possibilities to further one's knowledge or understanding of a greater whole beyond the physical existence."

Joe gestured back to Pete, who asked for any more hands. With none raised, he continued, "So now that we have a representation of life in the physical plane, moving up the sheet of paper through time, let's see how we can view nonlinear time. Frankly, it becomes simple. Once we hop off the piece of paper away from our present physical existence, we see many other pieces of paper, which represent both previous and future lives with their own scenarios drawn across the papers as their physical lives play out. In this state, we have the option not only to hop onto one of those papers to view the future or past life running but also to jump onto our piece of paper to view where our present was yesterday or will be tomorrow. It all exists in front of us from our perspective while off the sheet of paper or out of that specific life.

"An interesting quirk, though, is that we seem able to hop onto those other pieces of paper only where our future or past self is presently focused. We need the awareness of that other self where he is in his time in order to use his physical senses to experience that other time. We cannot view his past or future even though it exists, because his awareness is necessary to interact with that physical space-time. The same is true for the future self. He could jump to our time but is unable to see our tomorrow even though it is in his past, because our awareness is here now.

"An interesting thought, though, is that if he wanted to, couldn't he look up our tomorrow's newspaper in his past and find those lottery numbers? That rare instance when tomorrow's lottery numbers come to a person in a vision may be from accessing a future self who has seen the numbers, which would exist in his past. I propose a conundrum, though, that if he tries to view our tomorrow's lottery numbers, he can't, even though they are in his past, because they actually are not in his past until we experience them tomorrow. What we have not yet experienced is not available to him, precisely because such a situation would cause a loss of free will. Our tomorrow's lottery numbers depend on what happens from our present to the moment that they are drawn, so they do not exist yet, even for someone from the future, looking for them in his past. Until we experience their drawing, they do not exist. So here we have a situation where we can move through time to view our future incarnation's present, but within both of our lives, there is a role of linear time in each physical existence where the time in both of our futures does not yet exist.

"I hope you guys didn't get lost there, but basically, I am saying there can be movement through nonlinear time, but when viewing each physical moment of those other times, they all still seem ruled by linear time.

"Give me a moment here, but I have been sort of thinking on my feet as I am going along. I do think that it has happened that there has been an occasional instance where in a vision, a person has seen and learned tomorrow's lottery numbers, but it is not through the mechanism that I have described so far. Let me propose a second mechanism, which really should be a discussion on its own, but I'll mention it briefly here. I will suggest that another way to access those numbers is through contacting a central source of knowledge available if one is in the correct state of being. What is unknown or secret to us here can be manifest there and available. We will explore this place more in depth at a later discussion, but here, all that is known or can or will be known is available, including those lottery numbers.

"Access to this place by accident or by an adept's personal motivation could bring an awareness of many things as yet unknown to us here, even those lottery numbers. Inspiration and invention can be born here too.

"This is not a part of our discussion of time, so I will not go further with it now, but I brought it up only to solve the continued question of how tomorrow's lottery numbers can be found.

"I will end here partly because I feel that I need a break. Bill, if you have anything to say, the floor is all yours." With that, Pete plopped back on the couch, grabbing his glass to have a drink.

Bill arose enthusiastically. "Well, let's just keep proposing myths until we find one that fits. I find this reasoning to be backward or retrofitting and is used often to decipher an unknown. Take the unknown as a goal, and then create a mechanism to explain its existence. There need be no great hall of invention because invention comes from someone knowing the tool that he has to work with and, with a spark of inspiration, coming up with a new way to use them to solve a present problem. It is nothing more. The inspiration can come in a period of contemplation or concentration or in a dream.

"Then this visiting a friend or future self in the future is invention too, the invention of a deluded mind, I think. Let's get real here. We don't have knowledge of the future because it is not here, it is yet to happen. Maybe someone can get lucky at times, and if the odds are in his favor, he can guess a possible future and get it right sometimes. But that doesn't mean he has seen it or lived it even if he somehow thinks he has.

"That drawing on a flipping piece of paper trick was cute, but it doesn't make anything real."

With that comment, Pete rose and aggressively gestured to speak. When Bill acknowledged him, he started energetically. "I went only four dimensions with the paper analogy just to include time, but if we wanted to, we could go a couple of more dimensions. Then we could see a much more encompassing universe where all exists as one and our all is here and now. Our universe is much stranger than we, inhabitants and observers of the lower levels, can contemplate with the limited tool or brain given to us to interact with it.

"Our brain is a physical tool given to us to interact with our physical environment, and for that purpose, it does quite well. It has not, however, evolved to help us much with the nonphysical, ethereal aspects of existence. It has just enough capability to contemplate those points if we so desire.

"Thank you for allowing me to get that out just to confuse us all even more." More relaxed, Pete sat back down, satisfied.

Bill shrugged a bit and replied, "Well then, we have either a time scholar in our midst or someone who may be losing it." That brought a mild chuckle from the group. He added, "I, for one, when I am hungry, still walk to my car, drive it to the store, and buy something to eat. Food doesn't appear by dreaming it up. I have to go get it.

"With that, I am going to close with this: Time is what it is. We have been living with it and in it for our twenty-plus years and are getting by. More importantly, our existence makes sense. We know where we have been by our memories, know where we are now, and contemplate what our future holds and, more importantly, what we can do with our future. There is no getting that. I am done here and give the floor back to Pete for anything else he has to say." He gestured toward Pete with a nod and sat down.

Pete stood and began, "I thank everyone, especially Joe, for letting this evening happen, but before I finish, I want to relate a couple of small incidents that I have experienced myself.

"First, if you think about it, these may have happened to you too. I had a dream, one early morning, with a scenario which led up to someone shooting a gun. I was startled awake by the dream, only to hear, a second or two later, the sound of a car backfiring. This noise obviously occurred after the dream of the gunshot, but the sounds were identical. I had actually heard the backfiring car before it happened and interpreted it as a gunshot in the dream that was leading up to the gunshot. So somehow, I tapped into that backfiring car before it happened and built a dream story leading up to the gunshot to interpret the noise. So I had accessed the future in some small way.

"This, to me, is what is called a crack in the time continuum or a vision of a near future ahead of the flow of time as we interpret it.

"Another incident that happened to me was when I was in high school, even before I was interested in time as a subject to investigate. I had been an avid collector of insects as a hobby in my early years, but one day, when I got home from school, after my mile-long walk from school, I was looking in the mirror. When I found a bug in my hair, it was something I had not even seen before and did not ever remember coming across it in my bug books. It was a black ladybug with two red spots on its back. I looked it up in a book that I had, and it was named *Chilocorus stigma* or blood-spotted black ladybug.

"I then remembered a dream from the night before where I was under a tree filled with these same ladybugs. This was either a very unusual coincidence or I witnessed another crack in time. I took it as that and probably stored that away to maybe unconsciously push me toward more thoughts and interest in the possibility of randomly confronting the future if one is open to it.

"I want us all, if we get anything out of our discussion, to be a little more open to that possibility that time may just be a bit more complicated than we take it in our day-to-day processing of our existence here, and maybe at times, we can catch that ripple in time.

"I am, with that, probably to some of you, finally done here and again thank Joe for his hospitality and warm friendship this evening." He shook Joe's hand and sat back down.

Joe rose, saying, "Thanks to our participants and attendants, I thoroughly enjoyed tonight's discussion. It is getting late, so I will just suggest our next topic, and I think we should take some time next time and look more deeply into the idea mentioned here of that great hall of knowledge or source of what we sometimes call inspiration or an enlightened moment. Let's delve into what that place could be and what it offers. And here, I will wish everyone a good night, and I'll see you guys in the morning."

Except for Anna and Mary, everyone got up, donned their jackets, and with final good-byes, walked out. Anna said, "Joe, Mary and I decided to stay a few extra minutes to help you clean up. With the two of us, it shouldn't take long. Why don't you just relax and have that last bit of sangria?" Joe agreed and sat down while they got to work.

With everything straightened up, Mary came over to Joe and said, "I have to get going because I need to clean myself up a bit before I get to work tonight, so I'll see you guys later." Anna, who was near Joe, reached for his hand as he stood up, and they both said good-bye to Mary. Joe added, "I'll catch you in the morning before you leave work." Then he turned to Anna, and they wrapped an arm around each other as Mary departed.

Mary turned to face Anna and said, "Anna, you are a lucky woman. Joe is a very good guy. I would be after him if he didn't have you in his life. Joe, don't let that go to your head, because you are very lucky too. I am happy that you two have each other."

Joe replied, "Thanks. I know that wherever we go or she takes me, I am going to hang on tight to Anna."

Once Mary left, Anna told Joe, "I can stay a little while, but I want to get into work early, because once I am finished there, Marilyn wants to check out a couple of reception rooms for the wedding dinner with me, and she wants to start looking at wedding gowns tomorrow." They sat and listened to some more music while they just relaxed comfortably in each other's arms with occasional kisses and small talk for a while.

Chapter Eight

A Quiet Day

Five-thirty seemed to come too quickly for Joe. Even though it was a Saturday, he wanted to get to work or the floor before seven, so it was time to get his day started. He thought about the night before and felt satisfied with the way the discussions were going. He also felt that the gang was enjoying the meetings together.

While in the shower, he indulged in his memory of having Anna there in the shower with him. He also briefly thought of Mary and looked forward to a few minutes with her to see what she thought of last night's gathering.

All cleaned up, dressed, and with a couple of leftover tapas downed, he got into his car to make his way to work. He found the emergency room pretty quiet as he walked through and made his way up to the floor with a cup of hot tea in his hand for Mary.

Once he arrived, he found Mary in a corner cubicle, going over a few charts to make some entries before her shift changeover. She greeted him warmly and accepted the tea with a smile. She then said, "Joe, thanks for inviting me to come last night. I really enjoyed it. You certainly went beyond my Catholic upbringing, but I have wondered about some doctrines of so-called truths that we are told. And certainly, the ideas about time cause a person, if willing to be open to it, to rethink some things."

Joe replied, "I am glad you got something out of it, but remember, none of these ideas is easily proved. I do tend to lean toward believing in time being nonlinear in the greater scheme of things. I hope you will come again."

Mary answered, "I will." Shuffling some papers, she added, "Let me tell you about a new patient in room 17, a Mr. Barnes. He came in with a fever. He was cultured and started on broad-spectrum antibiotics. Otherwise, things stayed pretty calm last night, but I am ready for a little sleep when I get home soon."

Joe thanked Mary and felt pleased that she had enjoyed herself the night before. He said good-bye and went to see if any early labs were back and then stopped in to see Mr. Barnes briefly to introduce himself before going to find his crew.

Joe was hoping to finish work and get out by noon because he wanted to spend some time at the library and to check out some ideas on his computer, regarding both the great hall of knowledge and other topics regarding between-life activities. He also had some ideas about other future discussions. Then, too, he wanted to get to the grocery store for a few extra things to complete his dinner menu, because Anna was coming over later to dine and watch a movie. He hoped he wasn't too boring for her, but she seemed to enjoy spend the evening at home with him, and they did go out sometimes. He just found her company enjoyable and felt that it was easier to talk with her at home. Besides, he enjoyed the cooking at home.

Joe found his research to be fairly productive. He realized that the discussion about the hall of knowledge was going to be about what knowledge is there as well as if the hall does exist. He also looked into another idea that would change the perspective somewhat away from time and reincarnation by looking at what life's real purpose is. More specifically, is life's purpose here to learn something or just to live it?

Putting these things aside, he got to the store to get what he needed to complete his planned dinner. Then he stopped to pick up a couple of movies for them to choose from and continued home to get dinner started.

Anna arrived to the friendly odors of dinner cooking and, seeing Joe, gave him a warm embrace, accepting a glass of wine he offered her. She sat down while saying that Marilyn had worn her out that afternoon, adding, "I wished I had more work to do this morning so she couldn't get a hold of me so early. She wore me out."

Joe chuckled, "And many more days like that to come, I am sure. You two deserve each other. I am glad I am just the guy in this venture."

She frowned playfully. "Yeah, you guys get away easy on this marriage thing. What if we just elope?"

He laughed, "Right, like your mother would ever talk to you again."

She retorted, "Maybe that wouldn't be such a bad thing. So what's on the menu tonight, and what will it cost me?"

He answered, "Stuffed sole. And it won't cost you any more than you are willing to offer."

With that said, they looked deeply at each other and kissed briefly. Each took a sip of wine, and while she relaxed back into the couch, he turned back to the kitchen to check the fish, start some wild rice, and prep his asparagus.

While they enjoyed dinner, Anna filled Joe in about her day, both at work and with Marilyn. With dinner finished, they sat back on the couch, arm in arm, and watched a movie, occasionally sipping their wine or sharing a kiss.

Once the movie was over, they moved to the bedroom and cuddled together for a good night's sleep.

Morning came, and they both prepped for their day. After they were ready to face their day, they said their good-byes and set off to tend to their charges, Joe his group of patients and residents, and Anna her research specimens.

Mr. Barnes had been found to have diplococci on a gram stain of his blood, so his antibiotics were changed to a more specific treatment, and after repeating his chest x-ray since his admission, a patch of pneumonia started to appear to explain the site of his infection and source of his fever. He did well and was ready for discharge after a few days.

The ensuing days continued on with their occasional surprises for Joe but nothing that couldn't be handled. Joe had asked Paul if he could argue against the existence of a central hall of knowledge for their meeting, and he decided to argue the case in favor of such a place. The two of them set about their tasks of finding support for their arguments while they went about their usual patient-care work.

Chapter Nine

Meeting Four: The Great Hall of Knowledge

The morning of the next meeting came around, and Joe found himself looking forward to it. Whether some would call it useless diatribe, he found himself enjoying the discussions as well as just getting together with the others for fun conversation and interaction. The relatively quiet midmorning allowed him a little time to contemplate tonight's discussion. Anna had chosen to take up the talk in favor of a place that held secrets available to a worthy seeker while Paul was taking the other side. Joe had been involved in some of Anna's presentation but also knew of some of Paul's points of view, so he anticipated a good get-together.

The day had proceeded without any major incidents, so he and his crew were able to get away at a reasonable hour and agreed to meet at his place around 7:00 PM. He had time to pick up some beverages and went ahead and ordered pizza, a regular resident staple, again to aid in keeping the energy flowing.

Seven o'clock came around, and people began to arrive and greet Joe and Anna, who had come earlier to help prepare the place for the group. Once everyone was settled back and relaxed with something to eat and drink, Joe opened the meeting, saying, "Once again, I welcome everyone for what, I think, will be an interesting discussion regarding a place purported by some to exist called the great hall of knowledge, where answers to questions posed here can be found. My partner-to-be in life has agreed to argue in favor of such a place while Paul has accepted the hapless task of going against Anna, which I never recommend, and will argue against its existence. I am sure that everyone knows that I would be remiss, not to say in the doghouse here, if I don't leave this floor to Anna for her opening remarks. So, Anna, go at it."

Anna arose, saying, "Thank you, kind sir, and as always, thank you for your hospitality. I will get started with a few general remarks and then give the floor to Paul. Where does invention come from? Think about those first inventions—the wheel, the ability to communicate especially nonconcrete ideas or record thoughts or numbers onto a document, the steam engine, Edison's lightbulb, science fiction's faster-than-light warp drive. Interestingly, though to travel faster than light is theoretically impossible, I have heard of an occasional case of an astrophysicist seeing something supposedly moving faster than light. These inventions may be a natural extension of a person's knowledge in his field, like a surgeon using a tool available for one task in a new way to complete another task.

Or maybe these inventions, in a way known or unknown to them, were accessed in a place that gave them a solution to a problem that they were contemplating. Whether in a dream or in a state of meditation, did they access a great hall of knowledge that had an answer to their problem? With that said, I am going to give the floor to Paul." Anna sat back on the couch next to Joe and grabbed his hand for comfort. He gave her a smile of appreciation.

Paul stood and replied, "I am not sure that I am going to so much completely debunk this site of inspiration but maybe paint it in different colors and suggest other possible origins for the inspirations that Anna alluded to. It is quite possible that there exists a space beyond our usual sphere of general knowledge that can be a source of inspiration when we need a helping hand to progress from a surgical tool used in the intended way to using it in a new way. Or maybe that is just a built-in mechanism afforded us *Homo sapiens* to adapt to new situations.

"When the prehuman species depicted in the early part of Stanley Kubrick's movie *2001: A Space Odyssey* picked up that bone and threw it into the air, was that because he had touched the black monolith, or was his brain malleable enough to find a new use for the bone, to hunt or fight with it? Some birds pick up sticks to fish insects out of holes in the ground, and otters use stones to break open clam shells. Finding a new use for something in one's environment need not involve a trip to some place where a new knowledge is bestowed. It may be just the action of a creative mind.

"Let's see if Anna can come up with some better examples of use of an outside source of knowledge. I give the floor to Anna." Giving a gesture her way, Paul nodded and sat back down.

Anna got back up off the couch and began, "Let's take a different look at this. Who here has heard of Edgar Cayce?" A couple of hands went up.

She continued, "Edgar Cayce was a simple man who, in his younger years, slept at night with his Bible under his pillow. He began having spontaneous visions, and later on, with the help of others sitting at his side and recording what he said, he did readings on several subjects including God, religion, and reincarnation. However, he also did many readings while in a trance state about people's health. A person need not be near him, but he could describe the person's ailment and tell him that what he needed to cure him could be found on a particular shelf in the back of a pharmacy in the person's own town. Without even seeing the person or visiting his town, he could relay what was needed and where to find it to effect the person's cure. Paul, can you explain a mechanism for that without involving some central source of knowledge accessible somehow to Mr. Cayce?" She sat back down.

Paul regained his feet and replied, "Okay, so we need another mechanism for what Anna just related. I'll give three, and you guys can pick which one you want.

"Let's start with the first possibility, that great hall of knowledge. Does it have a street address? Because I might want to go there and check out a few questions, over an afternoon, that I have about some things. If it has all the answers to any question we could think of, then why is it staying hidden from us? Come on, life could be so much easier if we had access to answers for some of those questions, like why or what is life's purpose? If this place also has the answer to a particular cure for a person's ailment, then why is it so hidden? Why do we flounder around here searching for an elusive cure when the answer is just past that building's door? It would seem to me to be a mercurial god or his designee would have to be the curator to decide on who, coming to their door, would be given access to the information contained in their archives as was, supposedly, Edgar Cayce so allowed.

"Why would this place be such a secret if it really existed? We would need to invoke a reasoning that makes no sense, such as we are, in general, not worthy of access to such a place as long as we are existing as human beings. To me, that seems a bit arbitrary for an all-knowing, loving god to decide. If we are supposed to make the best of our lives, then why can't we get information freely at times when our lives are at a crossroad? Or isn't that the true question and answer? It is not for us to have access to answers to problems, mental or physical, posed to us in our present lives? And if so, what really is the purpose of this great hall of knowledge except to tell, once it's too late, what we could have or should have done to continue on our path of greatest spiritual learning to go on further? Make me a hall of answers, and then don't let me in, just lock the doors. If we are not let in freely to use its fund of knowledge, then it might as well not exist except for those few who may seem to have access to it.

"Let's move to a second possibility for Edgar Cayce's supposed ability. That is the possibility that mental telepathy exists. Though I may not want to give this much away, it may be necessary to do so to argue against the great hall. If telepathy exists, then Edgar Cayce's access is just to someone who knows where that medicine for a cure exists. It need not involve a greater central source. If Mr. Cayce could access the mind of someone who knew what chemicals he had in his backroom and what they were useful for, he could, by telepathy, find that medicine needed to effect a person's cure. He would not need a central source of all knowledge. To give you *telepathy* bothers me. What if he was just a good observer and remembered what he had once seen on a jaunt through a particular town? Granted, he gave readings on other topics including evolution, ancient history, and the existence of the soul, but those can just be a person's musings."

Anna jumped up, interrupting. "Telepathy, however, does not answer the problem or situation where a person wakes with lottery numbers for the next drawing. Theoretically, the numbers don't exist and can't be in the hall, but a person can say he or she has dreamed them. This would mean that there has to be access across time to find these numbers before they are picked in our future. Telepathy cannot explain this. The great hall must have information available, which will become available here only in our future. Thus, an invention spawns from a new idea or information. Can good luck once in a while plus a malleable open-mindedness be enough to explain the report of getting lottery numbers in one's sleep or known mechanisms for a tool combined for a new use, inventing a new concept or solution to a problem?

"Finally, chance could be involved in answering a problem, but with incidents like Edgar Cayce's, accepting chance as an explanation goes way off or skews too far for a result to depend on the flip of a coin.

"There may be something to the saying, 'Let me sleep on the problem.' Though answers don't always come, I think we get some insights more often than plain chance would dictate. If these answers exist in a hall of knowledge or just lie in the ether somewhere is unimportant, but I think, the answers are there to be had if one is open to them and looking for them."

Paul, a bit taken aback, restarted, "Well, thanks for finishing and, at the same time, debunking my answer, but you have seemed to cover it pretty well. My question to you then is, how does one gain access to go mindfully to a place that has the answers to things that haven't happened yet? Remember, to get to tomorrow's lottery numbers, you would need to move across time as well."

Anna answered, "Funny how our subjects can get interconnected, isn't it? We already talked about future numbers too."

Paul retorted, "Okay, if you are going to give me telepathy, then I could construct a great hall of knowledge that contains all of humanity's known knowledge through that telepathy. To have access to the lottery numbers, though, would mean access to the higher self's knowledge, which is unbounded by linear time as well. This is why the knowledge is so extensive, because it has answers to any question asked of it, even results of events in the future, because it is in a space not ruled by our physical realm's rules of time."

Anna added, "It also has the hall of invention that has answers to questions posed to solve problems in our physical world when the correct question is asked."

Paul regained his composure and stated, "So we are, so far, at a place where telepathy could fill in answers to questions we pose, and through the ether, an answer comes from someone equipped with understanding or information to give an answer. Whether the answers still belong to that someone else or they reside in the great hall of knowledge, you say they are available if one asking is able to bring the answer to the physical world and act upon it."

Anna replied, "The problem with moving through time for future lottery ticket numbers is not addressed above. The only way to explain such ability would be to accept nonlinear time in this higher level of consciousness where past, present, and future can be viewed as our present is viewed on this physical plane. Paul, I don't think we can get all the answers with telepathy, because in theory, no one would know tomorrow's lottery numbers until they are drawn, but there may be an answer to that conundrum by invoking access to nonlinear time in the nonphysical world beyond our usual physical senses.

"Whether a person is a recipient of a future knowledge through a spontaneous crack in time or he/she has the ability to navigate those cracks for answers is not important. The fact is that we get occasional anecdotes of that crack opening, and someone has an answer. I don't see getting around that. The answers manifest themselves to the seeker of them whether in a great hall of knowledge or dispersed and available in the ether of the higher realm of existence in which we live generally unconsciously."

Paul replied, "I feel defeated but partly because we are invoking a place that can't be proven to exist, which makes it hard to argue against its existence."

Anna answered, "I am sorry. I know the reasoning for this place is somewhat circular, that is, if the information becomes available, a place must exist where it is available, and if the place exists, it explains the availability of the information. I am sorry that that has to come on faith of the outcome. I can't show you the great hall of knowledge, but there must be a source of those answers."

With that, Paul said, "Okay, I give in." Then he went to refresh his drink.

Some of the others followed Paul while Joe spoke, saying, "If anyone has anything to add, go ahead."

Chapter Ten

An Unusual Day

It was a bad morning commute. It had been raining for two days pretty much straight, several inches. As Joe drove to the hospital, he encountered several blocked streets with flooded viaducts. He turned his thoughts away from his upcoming day to ponder the causes of what seemed to be out of normal range now, compared to how the climate had seemed to be when he was younger. Sure, some rain, a few winter storms, and nice autumns seemed a usual winter, but lately, it just seemed to be changing.

He arrived and parked then came in through the ER again. It seemed quiet, which was good, because he was anxious to get to the floor and meet with his group. He had something on his mind that he wanted to suggest for the next get-together that they would have.

After his cafeteria stop, picking up the lemon and tea for Mary, he headed for the ninth floor. She was on her way out to clean up before starting a double nursing shift but accepted the tea with thanks and a smile. He then turned to find his group.

Joe began, "Let's get started and see how much we can get done before the pathology conference at nine AM. I hope we can get together for a bite at lunchtime, because I have a great idea for our next meeting. We were a bit unsure when we left last time, but I think that I have an interesting subject." With that said, they took off to see where the patients that they were caring for were, on their road to recovery or elsewhere.

It was midmorning, and Mary caught Joe in the hallway. "I am having a problem with Jerry, the young guy in bed 12A. He is very short of breath. Can you come and take a look at him?"

Of course, Joe went down right away and entered the room. The young patient looked to be in acute distress, having difficulty breathing. *A pulmonary embolus?* Joe wondered. He sat down at the patient's bedside and introduced himself.

The patient replied with difficulty, "I can't breathe."

Joe responded, "Are you having any chest pain?"

The response was, "Heaviness, I just can't get air."

Joe made a clinical decision and concluded that the patient was having a panic attack, mainly because his age and habit leaned heavily against a serious physical problem, and he decided to sit with Jerry for a while. "What do you do when you have free time?"

Jerry responded, "I like to fish when I can."

There was Joe's inroad. "Put yourself on a lake on a morning, your pole in the water, and you get a bite. Then you pull up a sunfish. Just think about it for a few minutes. What a better place to be."

Jerry seemed to be calming, his breathing slowing. Joe asked, "How are you doing?"

Jerry responded, "I think I am okay, thanks."

After a few more minutes of sitting, Joe felt that the situation was resolved while Mary appreciatively observed the interaction. With that solved, the day continued on more smoothly.

Once their workday was over, they regrouped at Joe's place to discuss the weather, our possible effects on the environment, and whether Gaia and the physical manifestations of God can be conduits for our affecting our physical, natural environment through pollution. Once they got together, Joe paraphrased their topic. "Another way to look at it is our effect on the environment through our overwhelming mechanistic, industrial effect versus the environment's effect on our collective lives."

Joe continued, wanting to bring up the negative feedback effects of our energy release on our planet—that is, our energy use negatively affecting our environment while weather change, with nature's energy release, appeared as a result of our actions as a group. "Do we affect the environment, or does the environment change us as a group of *Homo sapiens?*"

Joe then stated that he agreed with and believed that our effect on the earth was to change it by our existence. He asked for hands to vote, and almost everyone agreed that the environment was changing as a response to changes we were forcing on the planet. They agreed also that the changes were irreversible. Finally, they agreed that with the results being mostly unchangeable, they wouldn't spend much time on the topic except to make a statement that though it seems inevitable, things should still be attempted to reverse or, at least, slow down the changes happening.

Chapter Eleven

Reincarnation—Experiences of Life Between Lives

When the gang had a chance to get together for fifteen minutes during lunch, they decided that their next topic to discuss would be reincarnation. Do we reincarnate, and if we do, how and why do we do it? Ravi was going to take up the side for reincarnation, and Paul was going to take the side against reincarnation. They also decided to keep it simpler by discussing reincarnation between human souls rather than including transmigration between different species.

The next week, they got together at Joe's place again for a discussion along with delivered pizza. Once everyone was settled in their chairs or on a couch, Joe opened the discussion by saying that Ravi was going to argue for the presence of reincarnation while Paul was going to argue against the existence of reincarnation. He then sat down next to Anna, and Ravi stood.

Ravi opened by saying, "There are numerous discussions regarding reincarnation. A central theme of the Buddhist religion is reincarnation with the rebirths reaching toward the state of satori and its end of the cycle of rebirths. The path of enlightenment is strewn with lessons to help the soul reach this higher level of understanding and grace, which benefits the soul on its journey toward complete awareness.

"Another example regarding reincarnation is the Inuits native to Alaska. Their beliefs are so strong that when someone in their group dies, the things belonging to that deceased person are held until a newborn can recognize those objects, and they are given to the child as belonging to the previous owner. These things are then felt to have been returned to the reincarnated previous owner of the objects.

"There are also stories in the psychiatric literature of anecdotal incidents where a person undergoing hypnosis is regressed back beyond his birth to a previous life. The abundance of such examples speaks toward the validity of these stories of rebirth."

With that, Ravi sat down, stating, "I will yield the floor to Paul and let him talk himself out of these repeated reports of provable anecdotes in the literature."

Paul stood and replied, "Sometimes, there is so much in the literature that we can prove almost anything with a literature search. Why does it seem that those people who reincarnated are so often famous? There should also be average people reincarnating along the way as often as the famous people."

Joe raised a hand, and when recognized by Paul, he stood and stated, "When we think about reincarnation, we think about past lives, but I want us to also think about the time between lives—what happens then and what its purpose is. Paul, do you have any thoughts about these things?"

Paul answered, "The time in between lives is felt to be used to review the just-finished life, the lessons either learned or not taken advantage of to help us to further our understanding of the true nature of the previous life. It also allows time or extra review of the previous physical life to gain as much benefit from the existence toward further spiritual growth. The main activity during the time between lives can be used to plan goals for growth during the next physical incarnation. The soul/spirit then draws out a plan, which has the best opportunity for further spiritual benefit. Assimilation of the events of the previous incarnation is added to the great scheme or plan to integrate input from the last physical experience."

Joe then cut in and asked Ravi, "Do you have a view of the purpose of time between lives?"

Ravi responded, "Review of the lessons from the previous life as well as decisions for the next incarnation are included to help plan the next learning experience during this in-between-lives period so that the life learning experiences of the next life are optimized.

"All this review and preparation for the next life experience are utilized to set up a life plan for the best chance of getting the optimal benefit of the next life experience."

Paul responded, "So the life reviews are in place to use the previous experiences to enhance outcome and benefits of the next experience."

Ravi stated, "So the previous life experiences exist to help educate the soul about its ultimate goal toward a completion of physical life experiences and learning possibilities. The speed of the learning experiences varies for each individual, but in the end, all souls will have the opportunities afforded to each one of them."

Joe raised a hand again, stating, "So once again, we haven't gone so much toward answering the question of reincarnation as we did regarding the nature of the soul and the purpose of reincarnation. If anyone has any questions about our topic tonight, please raise a hand." With no hands raised, they decided to call it an evening and break up for the night.

Once almost everyone had departed, Anna again helped clean up a bit, and then Joe and Anna decided to have some quiet time together while they cuddled and watched some local news while in each other's arms. Anna had a morning presentation at work early tomorrow, so they decided to not stay together for too long. After the news, Anna said her good-bye with a few hugs and kisses between them. When she promised to call him after she got home, Joe walked her to her car to see her off.

Chapter Twelve

Teaching Rounds—A Case Study

Teaching rounds were going to be a little different this time, starting with an old case presentation by Sub. They sat down as a group, and Sub briefly presented a case for discussion. It was a case that Sub knew from several years ago, so they could work the case from the diagnosis backward to the first presentation of the symptoms.

Sub started relating a case of a young white male adult who presented with a shortness of breath, a widened mediastinum, and an elevated alkaline phosphatase.

"A mediastinal biopsy is positive for sarcoidosis and negative for TB or fungi. The patient has a history of alcohol abuse. Some initial labs show an iron deficiency anemia and mildly elevated transaminases."

Joe raised a hand and, once he was recognized, asked, "Are there any pulmonary changes?"

Sub responded, "Approximately six months after diagnosis, symptoms of dyspnea on exertion are present with pulmonary function testing showing lowered diffusion capacity at 33 percent with mild restrictive and obstructive lung disease. The patient was given an eight-month course of oral steroids at approximately one milligram per kilogram per day with some symptom improvement.

"Symptoms are minimal over the next several years with mild reduction of diffusion capacity and an improving chest x-ray. Also present for years is a five- to ten-times normal alkaline phosphatase. Any thoughts?"

Paul raised a hand. "Any other lab results?"

Sub responded, "There are times that the transaminases improve and normalize, and at times, the sedimentation rate is elevated to approximately five times normal. There is really nothing much else happening until fifteen to twenty years into the illness when ascites appears along with slightly higher alkaline phosphatases."

"Any diagnosis yet?" continued Sub.

Joe ventured a guess. "Gallstones, biliary tree tumor, chronic duodenal ulcer with scarring and partial obstruction?"

Sub continued, "The appearance of the ascites after fifteen to twenty years led to a chronic recurrent ascites that required a paracentesis every three weeks to help resolve the ascites symptoms. The ascites was negative for cytology, straw colored, and a transudate on evaluation."

Just as Sub was finishing the case presentation, everyone's on-call pagers for the ER went off. Joe suddenly had a very bad premonition.

Once Joe reached the ER area that he knew so well, he was caught by a nurse who was able to lessen the shock by telling Joe that the patient was Anna, who had been in a serious car accident. He went to work right away, trying to stabilize her though the injury was severe. Once her vitals were stabilized, she was transferred to the intensive care unit for further care, Joe not leaving her side.

Epilogue

At the time of printing this book, the etiology and medical course of the patient with pulmonary sarcoidosis are not yet resolved.

The sarcoidosis was first diagnosed twenty-five years ago and the consistent abnormal alkaline phosphatase since then suggests an active disease process since 1987.

The therapeutic paracentises began for relief of symptoms approximately six years ago. The onset of seizures began around four years ago, and the peripheral neuropathy with pain has been present for approximately five years.

A diagnosis of the liver disease by biopsy was inconclusive and will probably wait until the patient undergoes a liver transplant.

If you have an interest in the final diagnosis, you can email the author for a request to be notified by email once the diagnosis is known, most likely after liver transplant: edneu51@yahoo.com.

CPSIA information can be obtained at www.ICGtesting.com
Printed in the USA
LVOW12*0705010813

345689LV00001B/1/P